TOEIC

練習測驗（12）

聽力錄音QR碼（1~100題）

LISTENING TEST

In the Listening test, you will be asked to demonstrate how well you understand spoken English. The entire Listening test will last approximately 45 minutes. There are four parts, and directions are given for each part. You must mark your answers on the separate answer sheet. Do not write your answers in your test book.

PART 1

Directions: For each question in this part, you will hear four statements about a picture in your test book. When you hear the statements, you must select the one statement that best describes what you see in the picture. Then find the number of the question on your answer sheet and mark your answer. The statements will not be printed in your test book and will be spoken only one time.

Statement (C), "They're sitting at a table," is the best description of the picture, so you should select answer (C) and mark it on your answer sheet.

1.

2.

GO ON TO THE NEXT PAGE.

3.

4.

5.

6.

GO ON TO THE NEXT PAGE.

PART 2

Directions: You will hear a question or statement and three responses spoken in English. They will not be printed in your test book and will be spoken only one time. Select the best response to the question or statement and mark the letter (A), (B), or (C) on your answer sheet.

7. Mark your answer on your answer sheet.

8. Mark your answer on your answer sheet.

9. Mark your answer on your answer sheet.

10. Mark your answer on your answer sheet.

11. Mark your answer on your answer sheet.

12. Mark your answer on your answer sheet.

13. Mark your answer on your answer sheet.

14. Mark your answer on your answer sheet.

15. Mark your answer on your answer sheet.

16. Mark your answer on your answer sheet.

17. Mark your answer on your answer sheet.

18. Mark your answer on your answer sheet.

19. Mark your answer on your answer sheet.

20. Mark your answer on your answer sheet.

21. Mark your answer on your answer sheet.

22. Mark your answer on your answer sheet.

23. Mark your answer on your answer sheet.

24. Mark your answer on your answer sheet.

25. Mark your answer on your answer sheet.

26. Mark your answer on your answer sheet.

27. Mark your answer on your answer sheet.

28. Mark your answer on your answer sheet.

29. Mark your answer on your answer sheet.

30. Mark your answer on your answer sheet.

31. Mark your answer on your answer sheet.

Directions: You will hear some conversations between two people. You will be asked to answer three questions about what the speakers say in each conversation. Select the best response to each question and mark the letter (A), (B), (C), or (D) on your answer sheet. The conversation will not be printed in your test book and will be spoken only one time.

32. Who most likely is the UK woman?
    (A) A travel agent.
    (B) A bank clerk.
    (C) A warehouse supervisor.
    (D) A restaurant manager.

33. What is the man complaining about?
    (A) An order has not arrived.
    (B) A bill is not accurate.
    (C) An item has been discontinued.
    (D) A reservation was lost.

34. What does the manager say she will do?
    (A) Delete an account.
    (B) Speak to an employee.
    (C) Refund a purchase.
    (D) Confirm an address.

35. What are the speakers mainly discussing?
    (A) Hiring a receptionist.
    (B) Replacing some outdated equipment.
    (C) Hosting a colleague's retirement party.
    (D) Opening another business location.

36. What does the man say about the city of Barrington?
    (A) Its population is growing.
    (B) Its infrastructure is outdated.
    (C) It has a new mayor.
    (D) It has good public transportation.

37. What will the man do tonight?
    (A) Attend a dinner.
    (B) Film a commercial.
    (C) Visit a property.
    (D) Treat a patient.

38. Where do the speakers most likely work?
    (A) At a brewery.
    (B) At an advertising agency.
    (C) At an art gallery.
    (D) At an amusement park.

39. What is the man worried about?
    (A) Hiring qualified employees.
    (B) Correcting a invoice error.
    (C) Meeting a deadline.
    (D) Responding to customer complaints.

40. What does the woman tell the man to do?
    (A) Send an update.
    (B) Take a day off.
    (C) Revise an advertisement.
    (D) Schedule a meeting.

41. Why is the woman surprised?
    (A) A colleague is working late.
    (B) Some documents are missing.
    (C) A cost is higher than expected.
    (D) Some projects have been canceled.

42. What problem did Ethan have this morning?
    (A) He lost his keys.
    (B) He ordered the wrong item.
    (C) He had car trouble.
    (D) His mobile phone did not work.

43. What does Ethan offer to do?
    (A) Stay late.
    (B) Cover an expense.
    (C) Check some information.
    (D) Submit a receipt.

GO ON TO THE NEXT PAGE.

44. What is the main topic of the conversation?
  (A) A vacation request.
  (B) A staff workshop.
  (C) A client visit.
  (D) A marketing campaign.

45. According to the man, what recently changed?
  (A) An insurance policy.
  (B) A budget.
  (C) An event location.
  (D) A keynote speaker.

46. What does the woman say about Amber Digbee?
  (A) She has won an award.
  (B) She is interviewing for a job.
  (C) She used to work with her.
  (D) She read her book.

47. What does the man imply when he says, "It will be my first time overseas"?
  (A) He cannot answer a question.
  (B) He is interested in a job offer.
  (C) He should not be blamed for a mistake.
  (D) He is nervous about a change.

48. What does the woman say a mobile app is used for?
  (A) Personal budgeting.
  (B) Social networking.
  (C) Shopping.
  (D) Global positioning.

49. What will the woman give the man?
  (A) A staff directory.
  (B) A business card.
  (C) A book.
  (D) A voucher.

50. Where do the speakers most likely work?
  (A) At a school.
  (B) At a department store.
  (C) At a hotel.
  (D) At a factory.

51. What does the woman mean when she says, "Aaron has to attend a meeting at district headquarters"?
  (A) A co-worker cannot attend a meeting.
  (B) A deadline will be extended.
  (C) She is assigning an additional supervisor.
  (D) She thinks that more staff should be hired.

52. What will happen next month?
  (A) A training course will begin.
  (B) Some student interns will arrive.
  (C) Some renovation work will start.
  (D) A team will be reorganized.

53. Where does the conversation take place?
  (A) At a library.
  (B) At a museum.
  (C) At a performing arts center.
  (D) At an outdoor market.

54. What does the woman thank the man for?
  (A) Buying her a ticket.
  (B) Approving her registration form.
  (C) Giving her directions.
  (D) Finding her a seat.

55. What is scheduled for later in the day?
  (A) A lecture.
  (B) A concert.
  (C) A beauty contest.
  (D) A cooking demonstration.

56. What does the man want the woman to do?
(A) Validate a parking stub.
(B) Teach a dance class.
(C) Listen to some recordings.
(D) Repair some equipment.

57. Why is the man unavailable on Friday?
(A) He will be performing.
(B) He has a dentist appointment.
(C) He will be traveling.
(D) He will be visiting a client.

58. What does the woman recommend the man do?
(A) Find a new instructor.
(B) Park in a specific location.
(C) Pay with a credit card.
(D) Speak with a manager.

---

59. What department is the man trying to reach?
(A) Personnel.
(B) Information technology.
(C) Security.
(D) Engineering.

60. What does the man inquire about?
(A) An insurance claim.
(B) A parking permit.
(C) A vacation policy.
(D) A weekly expense.

61. What does the woman offer to do?
(A) Take a message.
(B) Register an employee.
(C) Contact a supervisor.
(D) Reserve a room.

Sender	Gwen Finch
Recipient	Joaquin Rizal
Date	September 22
Amount Sent	$900 US = $46,139 PHP
Fee	$15.50 US
Transaction Code	DT-01238

62. Look at the graphic. What information does the woman have a question about?
(A) The fee.
(B) The transaction code.
(C) The date.
(D) The recipient.

63. What is the woman concerned about?
(A) Who can sign for a delivery.
(B) What identification is required.
(C) Where a package can be picked up.
(D) When a transfer will arrive.

64. What does the woman say about the shop?
(A) It has a new owner.
(B) It is close to where she lives.
(C) It will have a sales event.
(D) It has been closed recently.

GO ON TO THE NEXT PAGE.

Magnolia Tree Size Chart				
Type	A	B	C	D
Height	24"	36"	48"	60"

65. Why does the woman want some trees?
(A) To improve the appearance of an area.
(B) To have a regular supply of flowers.
(C) To conduct some scientific research.
(D) To provide more privacy for a home.

66. Look at the graphic. What size trees does the woman choose?
(A) 24 inches.
(B) 36 inches.
(C) 48 inches.
(D) 60 inches.

67. What additional service does the man offer the woman?
(A) Waste management.
(B) Regular maintenance.
(C) Tree planting.
(D) Fruit harvesting.

NATIONAL NETWORKING CONFERNCE

REGISTRATION FEES

	Early (before June 15)	Standard (after June 15)
Students	$1,700	$2,200
Professionals	$2,300	$2,900

68. What department does the woman most likely work in?
(A) Product development.
(B) Information Technology.
(C) Sales and Marketing.
(D) Finance and Accounting.

69. Look at the graphic. How much will the company most likely pay?
(A) $1,700.
(B) $2,200.
(C) $2,300.
(D) $2,900.

70. What will the woman send the man in an e-mail?
(A) A confirmation number.
(B) A cashier's check.
(C) A travel request form.
(D) A conference schedule.

Directions: You will hear some talks given by a single speaker. You will be asked to answer three questions about what the speaker says in each talk. Select the best response to each question and mark the letter (A), (B), (C), or (D) on your answer sheet. The talks will not be printed in your test book and will be spoken only one time.

71. What is the topic of the seminar?
(A) Computer programming.
(B) Graphic design.
(C) Buying a used vehicle.
(D) Using the Internet.

72. What change did the library recently make?
(A) It purchased new computers.
(B) It extended its hours.
(C) It added a new media center.
(D) It reduced late fees.

73. What are listeners asked to do?
(A) Apply for a card.
(B) Complete a survey.
(C) Create an account.
(D) Select a desktop theme.

74. Where does the speaker most likely work?
(A) At a fitness center.
(B) At a wireless network provider.
(C) At a paper supplier.
(D) At an office furniture store.

75. What is the purpose of the message?
(A) To file a complaint.
(B) To offer an estimate.
(C) To suggest another service option.
(D) To ask for more time to complete a project.

76. What does the speaker ask Ms. Chavez to do?
(A) Send a fax.
(B) Sign a contract.
(C) Return a phone call.
(D) Submit a deposit.

77. Who most likely is the speaker?
(A) A court reporter.
(B) An architect.
(C) An accountant.
(D) A yoga instructor.

78. What would the speaker like to discuss?
(A) Reducing company spending.
(B) Utilizing office space effectively.
(C) Adjusting a tax return.
(D) Drafting a product proposal.

79. What does the speaker say he will do tomorrow?
(A) Take a vacation day.
(B) Attend a seminar.
(C) Meet with clients.
(D) Mail some forms.

80. Where is this announcement most likely being made?
(A) At an art gallery.
(B) At a department store.
(C) At an appliance warehouse.
(D) At a bicycle factory.

81. What problem does the speaker mention?
(A) Some customers have complained.
(B) Some materials are faulty.
(C) A shipment has not arrived.
(D) A business has opened late.

82. What are the listeners told to do?
(A) Come in early tomorrow.
(B) Print more copies of a flyer.
(C) Take a longer lunch break.
(D) Contact a manager.

GO ON TO THE NEXT PAGE.

83. What does the speaker ask the listeners to participate in?
   (A) A fund-raising activity.
   (B) A company picnic.
   (C) A training workshop.
   (D) A community art festival.

84. What will be available in the cafeteria this week?
   (A) Healthy menu choices.
   (B) Special desserts.
   (C) A donation box.
   (D) A sign-up sheet.

85. What does the speaker say about the next meeting?
   (A) New employees will be introduced.
   (B) Attendance will be required.
   (C) It will be in a different location.
   (D) A guest will speak.

86. According to the news report, what type of facility is being closed?
   (A) A vocational school.
   (B) A bus station.
   (C) A medical clinic.
   (D) A community center.

87. Why was the facility closed?
   (A) It was outdated.
   (B) Its program was not popular.
   (C) Its funding was eliminated.
   (D) It was in a remote location.

88. According to the news report, what do authorities fear will happen in the future?
   (A) More people will lack adequate health care.
   (B) Public transportation will improve.
   (C) The income of rural workers will increase.
   (D) Similar services will open in other areas.

89. What is special about the restaurant?
   (A) Its location.
   (B) Its service.
   (C) Its food.
   (D) Its design.

90. According to the speaker, what will happen on October 10?
   (A) A grand opening will take place.
   (B) A major renovation will start.
   (C) A new chef will start work.
   (D) A cooking class will be offered.

91. What will some guests receive?
   (A) Memberships.
   (B) Calendars.
   (C) T-shirts.
   (D) Maps.

92. What type of business was the advertising campaign designed for?
   (A) A bank.
   (B) A hotel group.
   (C) A real estate agency.
   (D) A restaurant chain.

93. According to the speaker, what was different about the advertising campaign?
   (A) A celebrity was hired to endorse a product.
   (B) A promotional period was extended.
   (C) Ads were posted on social networking sites.
   (D) Coupons were sent by mobile phone.

94. According to the speaker, what indicates that the advertising campaign was a success?
   (A) Positive survey results.
   (B) Product sample requests.
   (C) Increased foot traffic in retail.
   (D) More website bookings.

```
KTJB Morning Schedule
(9:15-10:00)

9:15      Headline news
9:20      Business report
9:30      Local news
9:35      Traffic update
```

```
Sales Representative
Meeting Agenda

Opening talk — Jeff
Marketing budget — Harry
Price increases — Maureen
Quarterly outlook — Diane
```

95. What is the purpose of the broadcast?
(A) To advertise a store opening.
(B) To report traffic conditions.
(C) To remind listeners of an election.
(D) To announce a city council decision.

96. What did local business owners request?
(A) A new parking structure.
(B) Additional street lights.
(C) An alternate date for an event.
(D) An advertising campaign.

97. Look at the graphic. What will the speaker most likely talk about next?
(A) Today's top headlines.
(B) The estimated cost of a construction project.
(C) Names of newly elected officials.
(D) Traffic conditions.

98. Why is the woman unable to come to the office tomorrow?
(A) She will be at a conference.
(B) She has a sales appointment.
(C) She is feeling ill.
(D) She is expecting visitors.

99. What does the woman ask Joseph to do?
(A) Give a presentation.
(B) Postpone an event.
(C) Verify some prices.
(D) Consult a colleague.

100. Please look at the graphic. In what order will Joseph give a presentation at the meeting?
(A) First.
(B) Second.
(C) Third.
(D) Fourth.

This is the end of the Listening test. Turn to Part 5 in your test book.

GO ON TO THE NEXT PAGE.

READING TEST

In the Reading test, you will read a variety of texts and answer several different types of reading comprehension questions. The entire Reading test will last 75 minutes. There are three parts, and directions are given for each part. You are encouraged to answer as many questions as possible within the time allowed.

You must mark your answers on the separate answer sheet. Do not write your answers in your test book.

PART 5

Directions: A word or phrase is missing in each of the sentences below. Four answer choices are given below each sentence. Select the best answer to complete the sentence. Then mark the letter (A), (B), (C), or (D) on your answer sheet.

101. This West Lake Avenue entrance will be closed until ------- on the parking garage has been completed.
(A) constructs
(B) construction
(C) constructed
(D) constructive

102. Glover Foods, Inc. ------- yesterday that it expects diminished revenue growth over the next year.
(A) announced
(B) has announced
(C) announces
(D) announcing

103. The legal documents that Ms. Lavery needs are on file ------- the county courthouse.
(A) above
(B) after
(C) at
(D) among

104. Axion's new line of electric vehicles features ------- exterior designs and advanced battery technology.
(A) attractive
(B) attracting
(C) attract
(D) attraction

105. The Pancake House is as popular ------- Walter's Diner in the southern parts of the city.
(A) either
(B) with
(C) as
(D) of

106. When Everest Outdoor Apparel has a surplus of certain items, the company ------- donates the items to local charities.
(A) regularities
(B) regularly
(C) regularize
(D) regularity

107. The candidate we select must be able to work effectively ------- alone and in group situations.
(A) the same as
(B) not only
(C) also
(D) both

108. Quartz Light Speed sales representatives are reminded to follow specific ------- even when servicing regular customers.
(A) guidelines
(B) behaviors
(C) records
(D) qualifications

14

109. For ------- printing quality, use compatible Icer inkjet cartridges.
(A) optimally
(B) optimizing
(C) optimal
(D) optimize

110. The company president ------- Ms. Iverson with securing the contract with Star General Motors.
(A) agreed
(B) congratulated
(C) demonstrated
(D) entrusted

111. Mr. Simon said that to finish the contract proposal on time, ------- must volunteer to stay late tonight.
(A) one another
(B) anyone
(C) no one
(D) someone

112. Ms. Walker ------- sold the benefits of her expansion plan, winning the support of the company's executive board.
(A) convincingly
(B) convincing
(C) convinces
(D) convince

113. *Radiate Monthly Digest* features news from companies ------- the alternative energy industry.
(A) onto
(B) next
(C) in
(D) during

114. The growth of Tyrus Industrial Corp. over the past three quarters has failed to meet shareholders' -------.
(A) expectations
(B) expectedly
(C) expect
(D) expected

115. Food producers are experiencing high demand for ------- soy-based products.
(A) themselves
(B) them
(C) they
(D) their

116. The oversight committee will be limited to seven members so that the group may follow its agenda more -------.
(A) efficiencies
(B) efficiently
(C) efficient
(D) efficiency

117. Hotel employees will be happy to ------- guests seeking a nearby restaurant or movie theater.
(A) locate
(B) conduct
(C) assist
(D) remind

118. Job candidates have been cautioned that the interview process is highly ------- and only two positions will be filled.
(A) competition
(B) competitive
(C) competitors
(D) competitively

119. The self-recharging nickel ion battery is the ------- of many years of intensive research and experimentation.
(A) product
(B) producer
(C) produced
(D) producing

120. Sales of Crager Lawn Chief riding mowers increase ------- during the spring and summer seasons.
(A) openly
(B) rigidly
(C) dramatically
(D) frequently

GO ON TO THE NEXT PAGE.

121. All employees are invited to ------- the reception banquet at 7:30 p.m. in the Biltmore Ballroom of the Royal Terrace Hotel.
(A) express
(B) admit
(C) perform
(D) attend

122. Cory Fountain is the ------- president of Star Steel Industries in the history of the company.
(A) boldness
(B) bolder
(C) boldest
(D) boldly

123. Before recommending investments to clients, financial consultants at Barron Stone consider ------- variables such as age, occupation, and income.
(A) quantified
(B) specific
(C) occupied
(D) accountable

124. Patients who cancel appointments ------- 24-hour advance notice are subject to a $50 cancellation fee.
(A) usually
(B) already
(C) without
(D) almost

125. All staff members are asked to shut down their computers when ------- the office to conserve energy.
(A) exit
(B) exits
(C) exited
(D) exiting

126. Although the ------- findings did not prove the fabric to be water-resistant, the later results did.
(A) initial
(B) present
(C) forward
(D) ahead

127. After attending a recent sculpture ------- at The Wyatt Museum, Derek Logan signed up for an introductory art course offered by the museum.
(A) portrait
(B) creativity
(C) exhibition
(D) message

128. Photo identification is required ------- all non-authorized visitors to the Blight Building.
(A) for
(B) which
(C) until
(D) despite

129. The Ardos operating system from Bridge Solutions will ------- users to automate numerous repetitive tasks.
(A) show
(B) allow
(C) avoid
(D) provide

130. Six people from the marketing and public relations departments at Stabb Creative are being considered for ------- to management positions.
(A) transmission
(B) openings
(C) advancement
(D) opportunities

PART 6

Directions: Read the texts that follow. A word, phrase, or sentence is missing in parts of each text. Four answer choices are given below each of the texts. Select the best answer to complete the text. Then mark the letter (A), (B), (C), or (D) on your answer sheet.

Questions 131-134 refer to the following advertisement.

Top Notch Landscaping

Top Notch designs and installs landscapes with all types of plants, using all natural materials to suit every garden no matter how big or small. Our designs have ------- modest urban gardens as well
131.
as large-scale projects commissioned by architects and property developers. -------. However, no single nursery can offer plants of
132.
all species and varieties. That is why Top Notch has developed close relationships with specialty growers who ------- provide us
133.
with the plants we need. Such resources give us the selection necessary to complete any -------. In other words, whatever your
134.
landscaping goals may be, we can make it happen.

131. (A) collected
    (B) planted
    (C) transformed
    (D) distributed

132. (A) We are here to solve your home renovation problems
    (B) For most projects, we use plants and materials sourced from our own nurseries
    (C) Some cities have specific usage ordinances
    (D) Under normal conditions, nursery stock is guaranteed for 30 days

133. (A) readiness
    (B) readies
    (C) readily
    (D) ready

134. (A) project
    (B) survey
    (C) study
    (D) form

GO ON TO THE NEXT PAGE.

| To: Staff |
| From: Lou Swift |
| Date: April 5 |
| Subject: Big News! |

Dear Staff,

Thanks for your dedication and teamwork! In case you haven't heard the big news, Swifty Lube will be ------- a new location this
135.
summer. This additional service center is currently under construction at the corner of Geary Street and Park Presidio Drive in the Richmond District of San Francisco.

We will be accepting applications for qualified auto technicians and sales positions ------- June 1. Paul Grisham, our hiring director, will
136.
personally review applicants' qualifications from June 2 to June 9, and ------- is scheduled to begin one week later. -------.
137.   **138.**

Cheers,

Lou Swift, CEO
Swifty Lube

135. (A) exposing
(B) opening
(C) moving
(D) changing

136. (A) according to
(B) with
(C) until
(D) following

137. (A) trainer
(B) training
(C) trains
(D) trained

138. (A) Contact Swifty Lube if you are still waiting for an appointment
(B) Access to the main entrance will be blocked by construction
(C) Feel free to share this opportunity with interested friends and family
(D) Make sure you have received all of the training materials before proceeding

Smith-Tyler Donates to Youth Center in Nashville

A spokesperson for Jabari Smith-Tyler ------- that the basketball

139.

star made a sizeable donation toward the expansion of the West

Nashville Youth and Recreation Center. "Without his generous

support," said Ibn Ali, director of the center, "we would have

been thwarted in our renovation plans going forward."

-------. Now, a new wing will be constructed on the north end of

140.

the ------- gymnasium. The building will boast an Olympic-sized

141.

swimming pool, state-of-the-art indoor tennis courts, and new

staff and administrative offices. Additionally, private locker

rooms will be located ------- the current youth lounge.

142.

139. (A) has confirmed
(B) will confirm
(C) confirming
(D) confirmation

140. (A) Youth Center attendance has decreased over the past few years
(B) The original swimming pool is being converted into a game room
(C) Mr. Jabari's performance at the gymnasium was outstanding
(D) The project had been delayed because of budget cuts

141. (A) scheduled
(B) proposed
(C) irritable
(D) existing

142. (A) instead of
(B) as far as
(C) adjacent to
(D) even though

GO ON TO THE NEXT PAGE.

Date: August 4

To: Daria Steller <daria@coolmail.com>

From: Hugh Lomax <hlomax@wixler.com>

Subject: Product recall

Dear Ms. Steller,

Thank you for your recent ------- of the Wixler Fire TV Gaming Edition
143.
Console. We are contacting everyone who has recently bought this product to inform them that certain models are being recalled for repair.

In these models, the processor that enables the digital conversion of analog signal is faulty. -------. Please ------- whether your console
144. **145.**
has this problem by checking the serial number on the bottom of the unit. If it begins with the numbers "087," a repair will be required. Wixler will pay all shipping costs for sending your Fire TV back to us. In addition, we will repair it free ------- charge.
146.

Thank you,

Hugh Lomax, Customer Service Manager
Wixler Industries

143. (A) response
(B) demonstration
(C) purchase
(D) review

144. (A) This defect will eventually distort the sound coming from the speakers
(B) This special feature is unavailable on some older models
(C) We hope you will enjoy your new home for many years to come
(D) It is covered in the troubleshooting section of the manual

145. (A) verification
(B) verified
(C) verify
(D) verifies

146. (A) at
(B) of
(C) with
(D) on

Directions: In this part you will read a selection of texts, such as magazine and newspaper articles, e-mails, and instant messages. Each text or set of texts is followed by several questions. Select the best answer for each question and mark the letter (A), (B), (C), or (D) on your answer sheet.

Questions 147-148 refer to the following advertisement.

Storm King Windows

Custom-fitted replacement windows designed for subtropical and continental climates

Serving Residential and Commercial Needs

Free estimates

Visit our showroom at: 447 Holly Street, Cedar Rapids, IA 66720

Monday through Saturday, 10:00 A.M.-6:00 P.M.

Joseph Kalani

Product Consultant

147. In what field is Mr. Kalani employed?
(A) Insurance.
(B) Cleaning and maintenance.
(C) Commercial advertising.
(D) Retail sales.

148. What is indicated about Storm King Windows?
(A) It is hiring new technicians.
(B) It has just renovated a showroom.
(C) It serves homeowners and businesses.
(D) It has just moved to Holly Street.

GO ON TO THE NEXT PAGE.

■ ■ ■ ■ Attention Library Users ■ ■ ■ ■

The current Book-a-Book on-site reservation process will no longer be available at the Fairhaven City Library as of October 1. We will be transitioning to a new online Book-a-Book system that will allow patrons to reserve library materials remotely from their own computers. The new system will be unveiled in mid-September.

Any requests for items in the current Book-a-Book system made before October 1 will be honored. However, these requests will not appear in the new system. As of October 1, any questions about the status of reservations made through the old system should be directed to a librarian.

We appreciate your patience during the transition period.

149. What is the purpose of the announcement?
(A) To attract new readers.
(B) To give notice of changes to a procedure.
(C) To invite patrons to an event at the library.
(D) To introduce a new staff member.

150. What will happen to existing reservations after October 1?
(A) They will be canceled.
(B) They will no longer be free.
(C) They will be viewable only by librarians.
(D) They will need to be reconfirmed by patrons.

Doug Gleason (12:32 P.M.)

Hi Kim. We just received a shipment of cucumbers from Equi Farms. Should I place the new cucumbers on top of our current stock? Or should I sort them so that the riper ones are in front?

Kim Pignato (12:35 P.M.)

Thanks for checking. We usually rearrange them. Ask Sara to show you how.

Doug Gleason (12:36 P.M.)

Got it. One more thing. Fuji apples are on sale this week. We may need to order more.

Kim Pignato (12:37 P.M.)

We'll keep track of sales and decide as the week goes on.

Doug Gleason (12:39 P.M.)

//Sounds good.//

---

151. Who most likely is Ms. Pignato?
(A) A server.
(B) A farmer.
(C) A store manager.
(D) A food distributor.

152. At 12:39 P.M., what does Mr. Gleason agree to do when he writes, //"Sounds good."//?
(A) Rearranging the cucumber display.
(B) Asking Sara to contact Ms. Pignato.
(C) Selling Fuji apples at a discount.
(D) Placing another order only if needed.

GO ON TO THE NEXT PAGE.

Starlight Industries Pairs Up with E&T Recycling Center

June 19—The computer technology company Starlight Industries just announced it will begin working with E&T Recycling Centers. This partnership will enable consumers to responsibly recycle computer equipment, at no personal cost, simply by taking it to a collection center.

"Used computers make up a rapidly growing waste source," said CEO Indira Kapoor. "As a major producer of computer products, we believe it is our obligation to reuse what we can and keep heavy metals out of the landfills. This is what prompted us to go forward with this initiative."

Starlight Industries originally sponsored two pilot E&T collection sites and, given their success, aims to add ten more sites by year's end. To learn more about the initiative and for a map of current and proposed collection sites, visit ETrecyclingcenter.com.

---

153. According to Ms. Kapoor, why did her company partner with a recycling firm?
(A) To manufacture more affordable computer products.
(B) To follow a government environmental policy.
(C) To meet a responsibility as an industry leader.
(D) To pursue a rewarding financial opportunity.

154. What is stated about collection sites?
(A) They are not getting as much use as expected.
(B) They are no longer accepting volunteers.
(C) Their sanitary requirements are very strict.
(D) Their locations can be found on an online map.

Chef and lifestyle coach Lana Watson has announced her first foray into cosmetics with the launch of a new skin care business. Her Summer Garden skin care line consists solely of products made from organic ingredients and features extracts from plants, fruits, and vegetables. — [1] —.

"I've always served the healthiest possible food in my restaurant," said Ms. Watson. "Natural ingredients nourish our health and beauty from the inside out.

— [2] —. My skin care line utilizes only the vitamins and proteins in foods, such as spinach and cucumber, and combines them to create powerful moisturizers and cleansers that are free from artificial chemicals. — [3] —."

Summer Garden products are suitable for those with dry, sensitive, or combination skin and will be available online and at select retail stores beginning this September. — [4] —.

155. What is the article mainly about?
- (A) Local organic farms.
- (B) Online shopping trends.
- (C) A new business venture.
- (D) A company merger.

156. What is indicated about Summer Garden products?
- (A) They are suitable for all ages.
- (B) They are available for purchase now.
- (C) They are relatively inexpensive.
- (D) They contain no artificial ingredients.

157. In which of the positions marked [1], [2], [3], and [4] does the following sentence best belong?
"It seemed logical to create the products to nurture our skin from the outside in."
- (A) [1].
- (B) [2].
- (C) [3].
- (D) [4].

GO ON TO THE NEXT PAGE.

To:	Department Managers
From:	Margaret Langley
Date:	December 27
Subject:	Extended absence greeting
Attachment:	Sample message #5

Dear Managers,

In preparation for the upcoming holiday, when offices will be closed, I'd like to remind you that company policy requires each of our departments to replace the traditional greeting on their voice messaging systems with an extended-absence greeting that will play next week when callers are diverted to voice mail. This will involve making a new recording, saving it to the system, and programming the system to activate the recording at the close of our business day on Friday. Once you activate the extended-absence greeting, it will override the traditional greeting through the holiday.

The attached document contains the text of the greeting you should record. This is the same text we have used in the past, but as usual, the dates have been changed to reflect the current closure. Please use this document to record your holiday greeting. Make sure you activate it before you leave for the day on Friday.

158. What is the subject of the e-mail?
(A) A newly established company policy.
(B) An improved way to access voice mail.
(C) A procedure related to a holiday closing.
(D) A change to the traditional shift schedule.

159. What is included as an attachment?
(A) A script to be read aloud.
(B) A flyer announcing a company event.
(C) Instructions for installing a new phone.
(D) Transcripts of recorded customer calls.

160. What is indicated in the e-mail about the attached document?
(A) It is ready for publication.
(B) It is distributed annually.
(C) It is handed out to customers.
(D) It is intended only for new employees.

Around Town
By Charmaine Snyder

(August 10)—Robbin's has been a fixture on Bennington Street for over 80 years. The department store also served as Frederick Atkinson's entry into the working world when he was a teenager.

For three years, after school and during school holidays, Mr. Atkinson worked first in the stockroom and then on the sales floor, earning money for his further education. Now he's been hired by Ernesta Costa to give the store a new look. Ms. Costa, who happens to be store founder Lloyd Robbin's granddaughter, says the store is doing well with business from both residents and tourists, but she feels it needs updating. "I interviewed several designers and was particularly impressed with Fred's ideas. The fact that he already had a deep knowledge of the store was a definite plus," said Ms. Costa.

Mr. Atkinson's concept will preserve many of the classic touches of the old store. For example, the beautiful carved doorway and marble stairway at the main entrance will not be replaced. On the other hand, the showrooms will be redecorated, and the fitting rooms will be upgraded. The store will remain open during the process, and a grand reopening event is scheduled for the second week of October.

161. What is the purpose of the article?
(A) To advertise employment opportunities.
(B) To offer a profile of a new entrepreneur.
(C) To announce renovations to a business.
(D) To comment on tourism industry trends.

162. Who most likely is Mr. Atkinson?
(A) A university student.
(B) A tour leader.
(C) A store owner.
(D) An interior designer.

163. The word "touches" in paragraph 3, line 2, is closest, in meaning to
(A) modifications.
(B) features.
(C) contacts.
(D) sensations.

GO ON TO THE NEXT PAGE.

To:	mora.simmons@heltlx.edu
From:	e.agbayani@periodicalquest.com
Date:	February 28
Subject:	Periodical Quest

Dear Ms. Simmons,

This is a courtesy message to inform you that your monthly Periodical Quest membership fee for March could not be processed due to an expired credit card. To avoid any service disruptions, please visit periodicalquest.com/useraccount and update your billing information. If you have any difficulties, I will be happy to take you through the process.

Incidentally, while reviewing your account I noticed that you are not using our full range of services. As a member, you have unlimited online access to our library of over 3,000 journals, newspapers, and magazines. Additionally, as a professor you can also benefit from our resources for teaching and research purposes. It would seem that you did not complete your member profile when you signed up for our service four months ago. Please take a moment to review your member preferences. We want to make sure that you are taking advantage of all that Periodical Quest has to offer.

Feel free to contact me if you have any questions regarding your account. If you wish to cancel your membership, no further action is required.

Sincerely,
Elesa Agbayani
Periodical Quest

164. Why was Ms. Simmons contacted?
(A) A new service is now available.
(B) A payment was not processed.
(C) An order will be delivered soon.
(D) An article needs to be revised.

165. What is indicated about Periodical Quest?
(A) It charges a monthly fee.
(B) It has just doubled its journal collection.
(C) Its website is easy to navigate.
(D) Its customer support team is available 24 hours a day.

166. Who most likely is Ms. Agbayani?
(A) A magazine editor.
(B) A bank representative.
(C) A computer programmer.
(D) An accounts manager.

167. What is suggested about Ms. Simmons?
(A) She works in the field of education.
(B) She wants to cancel her membership.
(C) She has been traveling overseas.
(D) She has missed a deadline.

Chad Wallace Helps Toronto Go Green
By Steve Lee

TORONTO (May 8)—Members of the Green Toronto Society have announced the winners of this year's Eco Awards, to be presented at the annual Eco-Honors Banquet in July. This year's business prize will go to Toronto's very own environmentalist and entrepreneur Chad Wallace for his work in sustainable hospitality. Mr. Wallace opened the Wallace Inn in downtown Toronto just last year. — [1] —.

Its 50 guest rooms offer all the comforts of traditional accommodation but with minimal environmental impact. Solar panels, energy-efficient lighting, and smart indoor-climate control keep the building's energy use low. — [2] —.

Anton Wong, head of the Green Toronto committee, noted that Mr. Wallace was selected for the prize not only for making his business sustainable, but also for sponsoring cleanup days at Toronto's parks. He has even purchased eco-friendly sculptures for placement throughout the city as part of a municipal sustainability awareness initiative. — [3] —.

"Mr. Wallace recognizes that increasing awareness of environmental issues is not possible through regulations alone. We need to engage the community as well," Mr. Wong said. "Although he has lived here for only a year, we feel that he represents many of the goals that the Green Toronto Society is working toward." — [4] —.

---

168. According to the article, what will take place in July?
(A) A grand opening.
(B) An art exhibition.
(C) A celebration dinner.
(D) A park cleanup.

169. What type of business does Mr. Wallace run?
(A) A restaurant.
(B) A hotel.
(C) An engineering firm.
(D) A construction company.

170. What is indicated about Mr. Wallace?
(A) He supports community projects.
(B) He sculpts as a hobby.
(C) He holds a political office.
(D) He has a background in engineering.

171. In which of the positions marked [1], [2], [3], and [4] does the following sentence best belong?
"Even the property's decor consists of mostly recycled materials."
(A) [1].
(B) [2].
(C) [3].
(D) [4].

GO ON TO THE NEXT PAGE.

Questions 172-175 refer to the following text-message chain.

Rosa Gonzalez [10:02 A.M.] Hi, Anna. Ken and I are at the conference hotel. Where are you?
Anna Losch [10:05 A.M.] Waiting for a taxi at the airport. The traffic is horrible. It'll probably take me at least an hour to get to the hotel.
Rosa Gonzalez [10:06 A.M.] We ran into the same thing yesterday. I think there's road construction in the area.
Anna Losch [10:08 A.M.] Do you know when Vijay Rau is speaking? I'd like to attend his session on acoustic designs for office buildings.
Ken Yamamoto [10:09 A.M.] At 11:00 this morning.
Anna Losch [10:10 A.M.] //I won't make it.// Can one of you take notes for me?
Rosa Gonzalez [10:11 A.M.] I'm looking forward to hearing what Mr. Rau has to say, too. One of the offices I'm designing requires acoustic tiles.
Ken Yamamoto [10:13 A.M.] Actually, all sessions are getting recorded. You can watch his talk on the conference website later.
Anna Losch [10:14 A.M.] OK. I'll text you both after. I'll check in and drop off my luggage in my room.
Rosa Gonzalez [10:16 A.M.] I made reservations for us to have lunch in the lobby restaurant at noon.
Anna Losch [10:17 A.M.] Good, but it's going to be a working meal. We need to go over the slides for our design presentation so we have time to make any revisions.

172. Where do the people most likely work?
(A) At an airport.
(B) At an architectural firm.
(C) At a recording studio.
(D) At an event-planning company.

173. At 10:10 A.M., what does Ms. Losch most likely mean when she writes, //"I won't make it."//?
(A) Her flight arrived late.
(B) She did not reserve a room.
(C) Her presentation is not ready.
(D) She will miss a session.

174. What does Mr. Yamamoto indicate about Mr. Rau's session?
(A) It required advance registration.
(B) It is being rescheduled.
(C) It will soon be available online.
(D) It will be held in an auditorium.

175. What will the group most likely do at noon?
(A) Review a presentation.
(B) Attend a special session.
(C) Interview Mr. Rau.
(D) Check into a hotel.

Make Rock Star DJ the host of your next special event!

Rock Star DJ has been providing personalized musical entertainment services since 1999. While best known for its wedding DJ services, the company provides exceptional entertainment for teen dance parties, family celebrations, corporate events, bar and bat mitzvahs, music video parties, bar/club karaoke and trivia challenges.

WEDDING PACKAGES

All of our Wedding Packages offer an in-person planning meeting for that personalized touch. Choose from five packages (Ambience, Radiance, Brilliance, Vision, Concierge) and an exciting array of options. To see these packages and upgrades in action, please check out the videos on our website at https://wStardj.com./weddings

For those couples who appreciate the finer things in life, be sure to read about our recently launched "Concierge Package" that features live musicians and an incredible array of upgrades.

Add a Photo Booth to any package for just $899!

GO ON TO THE NEXT PAGE.

From:	Ned Rockland <nedrocks@rockstardj.com>
To:	Lorenzo Summers <losum@omail.org>
Re:	Your Wedding Package
Date:	June 12

Dear Mr. Summers,

Thank you for your payment of $3,389 for the Vision package plus Photo Booth. We appreciate your business, and it was an honor to be a part of your daughter's wedding on November 17. The video montage has just returned from the editing studio, which you can download it at: https:www.rockstardj.com/summers-frankel-wedding

In addition, your DVD copy will be sent ASAP.

You mentioned that you wanted to order digital copies of all pictures taken in the Photo Booth. We offer three options for Photo Booth Archiving.

Price List:
16 MB USB card — $99.99
32 MB USB flash drive — $139.99
784 MB Green-Ray DVD — $249.00

As for providing entertainment at your corporate meeting in September, I regret to say that we will be unable to accommodate you as we are completely booked through October. However, I'd be happy to refer you to an associated company who may be available on short notice. Let me know and I'll forward you her contact information.

Sincerely,
Ned Rockland
Proprietor, Rock Star DJ and Entertainment Services, Inc.

176. According to the advertisement, what can be added to any package for $899?

(A) A fog machine.

(B) A photo booth.

(C) A large video screen.

(D) A live band.

177. What is NOT mentioned in the advertisement as an event serviced by Rock Star DJ?

(A) Bar mitzvahs.

(B) Funerals.

(C) Corporate events.

(D) Trivia challenges.

178. What is indicated about the wedding that took place on November 17?

(A) It took place at Summers's corporate headquarters.

(B) It featured a karaoke competition.

(C) It was coordinated by Mr. Summers.

(D) It was captured on video.

179. What is included in the e-mail?

(A) Results of a customer survey.

(B) Descriptions of wedding packages.

(C) A practice schedule.

(D) A price list.

180. What does the associated company mentioned in the e-mail probably specialize in?

(A) Teaching music to children.

(B) Catering corporate events.

(C) Musical entertainment.

(D) Editing photographs.

GO ON TO THE NEXT PAGE.

From:	Luis Velarde
To:	Lily McVicker; Mercedes Watson; Doug Bo; Eric Hochhalter
Re:	Location Scouting
Date:	June 24

✉ Locations – 24kb (Attachment: Word Doc)

Hey Guys and Gals!

I thought we had a very productive business lunch at Pedro's Cantina yesterday. As the newest member of the Fiesta Restaurant Group, I am grateful to be part of the team that's opening the new franchising office in Austin. During our meeting, I couldn't help but notice our shared eagerness to expand FRG's business interests throughout the state of Texas.

I've listened to your suggestions and concerns about our ideal space and location for the new branch. Attached is a list and detailed description of spaces from www.haydenrealty.com that meet our basic criteria and budget. It's basically the best of the best; a short list of possibilities for everyone to look over. Please get back to me with your feedback and comments.

Luis Velarde, Fiesta Restaurant Group

4800 Landmark Blvd. Suite 500 — $2,000 (Travis Heights)

Open concept office/retail space in trendy Travis Heights; up and coming neighborhood with great foot traffic. Super "green" building; eco-friendly design will save you $$$ in energy costs. Building has underground parking. Suite includes four reserved spaces.

124 Red River Street — $1,900 (Hancock)

Elegant first-floor 1,000-sq. meter office suite with gated security. Located at Hancock Center, adjacent to St. Paul's Hospital. Just steps from subway station and three stops from downtown. Many high-profile tenants. Color copier/scanner/printer/fax on-site.

67 E. Cesar Chavez Street — $1,025 (Convention Center)

Free standing, multi-zoned. Former automotive service building. Can be customized to your requirements. High area traffic with Highway 183 frontage. Owner will lease or sell. The building is on 0.3 acres. Lot next door of 0.3 acres is also for sale. Located six blocks southeast of the Convention Center.

5775 Airport Blvd #400 — $2,000 (North Loop)

Fourth-floor offices. Adjacent city parking lot with discounted monthly permits for tenants. Building has security access controls. Located at ACC Highland Industrial Park. State-of-the-art Coldarrow video conferencing; 4G high-speed wireless Internet included.

GO ON TO THE NEXT PAGE.

From:	Eric Hochhalter
To:	Lily McVicker; Luis Velarde; Mercedes Watson; Doug Bo
Re:	Office Space
Date:	June 25

Dear Teammates,

First of all, kudos to Luis for taking the initiative and narrowing down our search to these options. It sounds like you guys made some major headway at the last minute. Sorry I missed it, but the situation at Pollo Paradise in Waco couldn't be helped. Since I'm the last to comment on this e-mail discussion, please be patient with me.

Mercedes, I appreciate your comments about being in a high-profile location with good transportation, but we can't lose sight of our priority, which is customizing a space to our specific needs. Is anyone familiar with public transportation in Austin? It would help to know if the building near the convention center has adequate public transportation.

I also agree with Luis's idea that we should make some inquiries down at the Austin Planning Commission about construction permits. I will try to look into it this weekend when my wife and I attend the Austin Music Festival with my cousin, Roger, who attended University of Texas and is very familiar with real estate in the area.

Eric, FRG

181. Why did Mr. Velarde send the e-mail?
(A) To follow up on a meeting.
(B) To confirm a reservation at Pedro's Cantina.
(C) To organize a business trip.
(D) To inquire about some real estate.

182. What is one property feature mentioned in the attachment?
(A) A loading dock.
(B) A popular restaurant in the building.
(C) A video conferencing system.
(D) A nearby recreation center.

183. Which property does Mr. Hochhalter most likely favor?
(A) 4800 Landmark Boulevard.
(B) 124 Red River Street.
(C) 5775 Airport Boulevard.
(D) 67 E. Cesar Chavez Street.

184. What is indicated about Ms. Watson?
(A) She just moved to Hancock.
(B) She is the newest member of the team.
(C) She sent an e-mail to her colleagues.
(D) She used to live in North Loop.

185. What is suggested about Mr. Hochhalter?
(A) He missed the meeting at Pollo Paradise.
(B) He is considering a divorce.
(C) He plans to attend a performance.
(D) He went to college in Austin.

Home Works

June 24

Mr. Richard Metzer

2390 N. Clark Street

Chicago, IL 60625

Thank you for being a loyal Home Works customer. Our records indicate that you recently made a purchase with your Home Works Advantage credit card. At the moment, we are conducting a brief survey about your Home Works shopping experience. The enclosed survey should take no more than five minutes to complete and we would deeply appreciate your feedback. A prepaid, self-addressed envelope is included for your convenience. And as a reward for your patronage, customers who respond before July 3 will receive a complete set of Ambrosia scented candles. Those who return a completed survey after that date will receive a coupon for 10 percent off of their next purchase.

Thank you in advance for your participation.

Sincerely,

Diana Williams

Home Works Director of Customer Care

GO ON TO THE NEXT PAGE.

CUSTOMER SATISFACTION SURVEY

Customer name: Richard Metzger

Date: June 28

Overall, how would you rate your shopping experience at Home Works?

Not satisfied		Satisfied	Very satisfied	
1	2	3	4	(5)

How likely would you be to recommend Home Works to a friend?

Not likely		Somewhat likely	Very likely	
1	2	3	4	(5)

Did you find what you were looking for at Home Works?

No	(Yes)

Which Home Works location did you visit?

Lincoln Avenue in Edgewater

Additional comments:

Home Works is my favorite household furnishing store in Chicago. The staff is extremely friendly and helpful, but I am most impressed by the incredible selection. I tell my friends that if you can't find it at Home Works, you probably won't be able to find it.

Additional comments:

---

186. Why did Ms. Williams write to Mr. Metzger?
   (A) To announce a private event.
   (B) To deny a refund.
   (C) To confirm an order.
   (D) To ask for some feedback.

187. What is indicated about Home Works?
   (A) It issues credit cards to customers.
   (B) It carries high-end merchandise.
   (C) It is opening a new location in Edgewater.
   (D) It is hiring sales staff.

188. What will Mr. Metzger most likely receive from Home Works?
   (A) A set of candles.
   (B) A discount coupon.
   (C) A follow-up phone call.
   (D) An extra set of towels.

189. In the letter, the word "appreciate" in paragraph 1 line 5 is closest in meaning to
   (A) be thankful for.
   (B) authorize.
   (C) dismiss.
   (D) disclose.

190. What does Mr. Metzger mention about Home Works?
   (A) Its products are often out of stock.
   (B) Its sales people are not helpful.
   (C) It has the lowest prices.
   (D) It has a wide variety of items.

EDUCATION REIMBURSEMENT PROGRAM

Argus Allied LLC's Education Reimbursement Program assists permanent employees who want to attain higher levels of professional skills and knowledge. Educational assistance may cover up to 75 percent of the cost of tuition. It may also be used for the completion of approved job-related classes leading to a degree from any accredited university. Course materials and other fees are not eligible for reimbursement.

Not all courses are automatically considered job-relevant. The Director of Human Resources will determine whether a course or degree meets the guidelines of the Education Reimbursement Program. Employees must submit a course approval form to the Human Resources Department before enrolling in a course in order to be eligible for assistance.

GO ON TO THE NEXT PAGE.

From:	Edward Bloom <e_bloom@argus.com>
To:	Molly Zhang <m_zhang@argus.com>
Re:	Approval for courses
Date:	Molly Zhang <m_zhang@argus.com>

✉ EAAF Approval Form – 13.9kb (Attachment: Word Doc)

Dear Mr. Bloom,

I am planning to take two courses at Hempford University during the upcoming semester in the evening program. At this rate, I should be finished with the Accelerated Master's Degree program by December of next year. I have attached the approval form to this e-mail. One of the courses does not have finalized dates yet, but I was **told** that it would start in early October. As soon as I get your approval, I will officially enroll in the courses online.

Thank you,

Molly Zhang

Educational Assistance Approval Form

Employee Information

Employee name :   Molly Zhang
Position :   Customer Care Representative
Division :   Customer Service

Work-related Class Information

Degree sought :   Master of Business Administration
Name of institution : Hempford University
Name of course :   International Finance
Course starting date : September 14
Course ending date :   December 9

Name of course :   Leadership Development
Course starting date : To Be Determined
Course ending date :   To Be Determined

---

191. How does the company assist employees with education?
(A) It lets employees work at home.
(B) It allows flexible work schedules.
(C) It pays for part of the tuition.
(D) It covers the cost of textbooks.

192. In what department does Mr. Bloom most likely work?
(A) Continuing Education.
(B) Product development.
(C) Customer Service.
(D) Human Resources.

193. When will the leadership development course most likely begin?
(A) In June.
(B) In September.
(C) In October.
(D) In December.

194. What is the purpose of the e-mail?
(A) To apply for permission to take classes.
(B) To promote a new educational program.
(C) To ask for a letter of reference.
(D) To suggest a change to a policy.

195. What is required to obtain educational assistance?
(A) The courses must be completed online.
(B) The degree program must be relevant to the job.
(C) The university must be affiliated with Juniper Allied.
(D) The employee must attend classes at night.

GO ON TO THE NEXT PAGE.

Questions 196-200 refer to the following advertisement and e-mail.

www.activeathletics.com

Home	Products	Support	Vendors

ACTIVE ATHLETICS ONLINE

THE #1 ON-LINE SPORTING GOODS RETAILER

Get pumped up!! with the best-selling

Proflex 5.1
Utility Weight Bench

THIS WEEK ONLY!!!!!
Unbelievable Price!

~~Order today,~~ use it tomorrow

$229.00 >>> $159.99*

includes taxes and overnight delivery

Take an extra $10 off with coupon code:

ACTIVENOW

"The Proflex 5.1 fully-adjustable weight bench is the industry standard in fitness centers across the U.S.!"
— Tom Johnson, fitness expert

This week only, save 30% on Proflex, the hottest name in exercise equipment! Our warehouses are jammed to capacity, so we're slashing prices and clearing our inventory in order to make way for the next generation of exercise equipment.

From:	Ace Derrick <ace_d@pueblo.com
To:	Active Athletics <customerservice@activeathletics.com>
Re:	Order Reference #EH-28934
Date:	August 16

This is the fourth e-mail I have sent in the past two weeks, and I have yet to receive a response or an explanation about the weight bench. I've also called the 1-800 number at least a dozen times, only to be put on hold indefinitely.

As evidenced by both the reference number and the confirmation e-mail you sent, I purchased the Proflex 5.1 from your website on August 1 using the coupon code. The website clearly stated that (a) the bench was in stock, and (b) it would be shipped overnight.

This is hardly the kind of service I would expect from the "#1 Online Retailer". However, I do expect one of the following two things to happen within the next 48 hours. Either I receive the weight bench, or you refund my money. Keep in mind that whatever happens, I intend to report Active Athlete to the Bureau of Consumer Fraud.

Please respond appropriately.

Ace Derrick

GO ON TO THE NEXT PAGE.

196. Why is the Proflex 5.1 Weight Bench on sale?
- (A) The company facing expensive litigation.
- (B) The company needs room for new products.
- (C) It has been replaced by a newer model.
- (D) It has been recalled by the manufacturer.

197. What does the advertisement NOT promise?
- (A) Online savings.
- (B) Warranty.
- (C) Taxes included.
- (D) Overnight delivery.

198. In the advertisement, paragraph 1, line 4, what is the closest meaning of "inventory"?
- (A) options
- (B) stock
- (C) storage
- (D) utility

199. How much did Ace Derrick most likely pay for the bench?
- (A) $99.99.
- (B) $139.99.
- (C) $149.99.
- (D) $229.99 plus tax and delivery.

200. What did Ace Derrick ask the company to do?
- (A) Contact him promptly.
- (B) Send a different model.
- (C) Give him store credit.
- (D) File a complaint with the bureau.

Stop! This is the end of the test. If you finish before time is called, you may go back to Parts 5, 6, and 7 and check your work.

New TOEIC Listening Script

PART 1

1. (   ) (A) They are servicing a bicycle.
   (B) They are searching a room.
   (C) They are washing a car.
   (D) They are towing a boat.

2. (   ) (A) The clerk is stocking the shelves.
   (B) The professor is giving a lecture.
   (C) The manager is interviewing a candidate.
   (D) The doctor is examining a patient.

3. (   ) (A) The fireman is climbing a ladder.
   (B) The teacher is closing a window.
   (C) The server is taking a man's order.
   (D) The mechanic is removing a tire.

4. (   ) (A) The taxis are waiting for passengers.
   (B) The buses are leaving the highway.
   (C) The trucks are parked on the hill.
   (D) The trains are leaving the station.

5. (   ) (A) Some people are attending a concert.
   (B) Some people are watching a movie.
   (C) Some people are leaving the train station.
   (D) Some people are sitting in a park.

6. (   ) (A) The woman is reading some documents.
   (B) The woman is typing on a laptop.
   (C) The woman is drinking coffee.
   (D) The woman is talking on the phone.

GO ON TO THE NEXT PAGE.

PART 2

7. (   ) What time does the next train to San Diego leave?
    (A) At the next stop.
    (B) In half an hour.
    (C) About 10 dollars.

8. (   ) Did you go to the doctor yesterday?
    (A) It's a new type of therapy.
    (B) Yes, that's why I left work early.
    (C) Some friends from school.

9. (   ) My car broke down on Fontana Boulevard.
    (A) OK, I'll send someone to pick you up.
    (B) It's about 20 miles.
    (C) Some new business cards.

10. (   ) The sale promotion was a big success, wasn't it?
    (A) Yes, it went very well.
    (B) By the end of the month.
    (C) He's at a conference in Los Angeles.

11. (   ) Do employees here receive weekly or bi-weekly paychecks?
    (A) Only a year-end bonus.
    (B) At the bank on the corner.
    (C) They get paid every Friday.

12. (   ) Where can I find the vacation request forms?
    (A) To Denver and Chicago.
    (B) A revised itinerary.
    (C) In the file cabinet by the door.

13. (   ) Please watch your step as you exit the building.
    (A) Sure, I'll be careful.
    (B) At the board meeting.
    (C) About 45 minutes.

14. (   ) How will I pay for dinner with the client?
    (A) Last night at 8 o'clock.
    (B) Business formal.
    (C) Use the company credit card.

15. (　　) Do you want to go to the concert tonight?
    (A) What time is the show?
    (B) A new guitar.
    (C) Charlie found one this morning.

16. (　　) When is the Thrask deal going to be finalized?
    (A) No, that was a good meal.
    (B) There's a collection bin on the second floor.
    (C) Their CEO's out of the country this week.

17. (　　) How did you hear about our consumer survey?
    (A) I read about it in the newspaper.
    (B) How can I help you?
    (C) That's where I'm going.

18. (　　) We should hire some workers, shouldn't we?
    (A) Yes, that's a good idea.
    (B) Friday afternoon at 3:30.
    (C) Fill out an expense report.

19. (　　) Why was the training session rescheduled for later in the day?
    (A) Thanks. It was a difficult decision.
    (B) At a location in the city center.
    (C) You'd have to ask the supervisor.

20. (　　) How long are you planning on staying at Coleman Industries?
    (A) For our upstairs neighbor.
    (B) I'm not sure of my future plans.
    (C) We work in the same department.

21. (　　) Are you interested in working an extra shift at the restaurant?
    (A) That customer needs a menu.
    (B) Thanks, we already ordered.
    (C) Which day would you need me?

22. (　　) Where is the accounting department located?
    (A) Here's the building directory.
    (B) Because it wasn't paid.
    (C) That seems low.

GO ON TO THE NEXT PAGE.

23. (   ) Traffic is going to be bad. We should leave soon.
    (A) I left it at home.
    (B) I'll be ready in a few minutes.
    (C) Visit the website.

24. (   ) Who are we putting on the magazine's front cover this month?
    (A) In the other room.
    (B) We'll decide tomorrow.
    (C) Yes, I wrote the article.

25. (   ) I think Leah Norkus will get the Employee of the Year award, don't you?
    (A) For dinner on Saturday.
    (B) About a hundred employees.
    (C) Probably. She deserves it.

26. (   ) On which websites should we publish our advertisements?
    (A) About 500 words.
    (B) Let's try some social media sites.
    (C) I read that already.

27. (   ) Why hasn't the maintenance crew cleaned up the clothing displays?
    (A) No, the printer is not working.
    (B) Yes, last Tuesday.
    (C) Because they were unloading a truck.

28. (   ) Aren't you gonna help me do the dishes?
    (A) I've been there before.
    (B) Sorry, I have to make an important phone call.
    (C) The second building on the right.

29. (   ) Should we inspect the machine shop this morning or this afternoon?
    (A) I got some new T-shirts.
    (B) Please put them in order of time received.
    (C) This afternoon is better for me.

30. (   ) Who will manage the quality assurance team after Candace leaves?
    (A) In the warehouse district.
    (B) I thought she decided to stay.
    (C) Tickets for the game are sold out.

31. (   ) The marketing department has a larger budget this quarter.
  (A) Now they can hire more staff.
  (B) He's a junior account executive.
  (C) Isn't Julie at the technology conference?

PART 3

Questions 32 through 34 *refer to the following conversation between three speakers.*

M : I beg your pardon, are you the manager?
Woman UK : Yes. Is there a problem, sir?

M : I ordered the chicken. My server Jenny said it would be out several times, but I'm still waiting.
Woman UK : About how long?

M : At least 25 minutes.
Woman UK : Oh, that's unreasonable. Let me find out what the holdup is. Jenny, this diner has been waiting nearly half an hour for his meal.

Woman US : I'm very sorry. I've asked the chef, but the kitchen is really slow tonight.
Woman UK : I'll ask the chef to send out your meal right away.

32. (   ) Who most likely is the UK woman?
  (A) A travel agent.
  (B) A bank clerk.
  (C) A warehouse supervisor.
  (D) A restaurant manager.

33. (   ) What is the man complaining about?
  (A) An order has not arrived.
  (B) A bill is not accurate.
  (C) An item has been discontinued.
  (D) A reservation was lost.

34. (   ) What does the manager say she will do?
  (A) Delete an account.
  (B) Speak to an employee.
  (C) Refund a purchase.
  (D) Confirm an address.

GO ON TO THE NEXT PAGE.

M : Sarah, I know you were excused from the staff meeting we had yesterday, so I wanted to fill you in. I'm planning to open another dental clinic. This one would be in Barrington.

W : Really? Wow! Though... doesn't Barrington seem a little close? It's only a 10-minute drive from this clinic. Will there be enough business for another location?

M : Yes, I wondered about that initially, but Barrington's an up-and-coming city. Lots of people are moving there. Plus, we found an unbeatable deal on an available space. I'll go there tonight so I can view the property again and possibly sign a lease.

35. (   ) What are the speakers mainly discussing?
      (A) Hiring a receptionist.
      (B) Replacing some outdated equipment.
      (C) Hosting a colleague's retirement party.
      (D) Opening another business location.

36. (   ) What does the man say about the city of Barrington?
      (A) Its population is growing.
      (B) Its infrastructure is outdated.
      (C) It has a new mayor.
      (D) It has good public transportation.

37. (   ) What will the man do tonight?
      (A) Attend a dinner.
      (B) Film a commercial.
      (C) Visit a property.
      (D) Treat a patient.

W : Good afternoon, Steve. How's the new beer bottle label design coming along? Don't forget, the client wants to see the final design by the end of the week.

M : The whole team has been working really hard. We've got the basic layout, but we still need to decide on the color scheme. I'm concerned that we might not be ready for Friday.

W : Your department always does great work. I'm not terribly concerned. Just please send me an e-mail on Wednesday letting me know your progress.

M: Thanks. OK, will do.

38. (　　) Where do the speakers most likely work?
    (A) At a brewery.
    (B) At an advertising agency.
    (C) At an art gallery.
    (D) At an amusement park.

39. (　　) What is the man worried about?
    (A) Hiring qualified employees.
    (B) Correcting a invoice error.
    (C) Meeting a deadline.
    (D) Responding to customer complaints.

40. (　　) What does the woman tell the man to do?
    (A) Send an update.
    (B) Take a day off.
    (C) Revise an advertisement.
    (D) Schedule a meeting.

Questions 41 through 43 _refer to the following question between three speakers._

W : Ethan, I'm surprised to see you still at the office. You usually get off at 5:30, right?

Man AUS : Yeah, but I didn't come in until noon today because my car wouldn't start. It's at the repair shop getting fixed now.

W : Oh, how are you getting home, then?

Man AUS : I'm waiting for Gerard. He lives in my neighborhood and he offered me a ride home. And… Here he comes now.

Man CAN : Hi, Ethan. I'm ready to go, but do you mind if we stop at the gas station on the way home? I forgot to fill up this morning on the way to work.

Man AUS : Sure. In fact, let me pay this time. It's the least I can do for all the times you've given me a ride.

41. (　　) Why is the woman surprised?
    (A) A colleague is working late.
    (B) Some documents are missing.
    (C) A cost is higher than expected.
    (D) Some projects have been canceled.

GO ON TO THE NEXT PAGE.

42. (   ) What problem did Ethan have this morning?
     (A) He lost his keys.
     (B) He ordered the wrong item.
     (C) He had car trouble.
     (D) His mobile phone did not work.

43. (   ) What does Ethan offer to do?
     (A) Stay late.
     (B) Cover an expense.
     (C) Check some information.
     (D) Submit a receipt.

Questions 44 through 46 _refer to the following conversation._

W : Leo, you're attending the technology seminar here at the office on Saturday, right? Do you know what time it's supposed to start?

M : Nine-thirty a.m. It will be led by an outside consultant, Amber Digbee. Oh, and the location has been changed from conference room C to the main conference room.

W : Oh, good to know. I'm really looking forward to the seminar. I used to work with Amber at my previous job.

44. (   ) What is the main topic of the conversation?
     (A) A vacation request.
     (B) A staff workshop.
     (C) A client visit.
     (D) A marketing campaign.

45. (   ) According to the man, what recently changed?
     (A) An insurance policy.
     (B) A budget.
     (C) An event location.
     (D) A keynote speaker.

46. (   ) What does the woman say about Amber Digbee?
     (A) She has won an award.
     (B) She is interviewing for a job.
     (C) She used to work with her.
     (D) She read her book.

W : Griffin, are you ready for your relocation to our Singapore offices?

M : It will be my first time living overseas. And I have to find an apartment and learn how things work.

W : Isn't the company helping you get settled?

M : Sure, but I mean other than our colleagues, I don't know anyone in Singapore.

W : Hey, there's a great mobile app you should get called 'Landed'. It will link you to a network of people who just moved to the city. Should be a useful social connection.

M : Wonderful, I'll check it out.

W : Also, I have a travel guide that I used on my last visit to Singapore which has some good information. I'll bring it in for you tomorrow.

47. (　　) What does the man imply when he says, "It will be my first time overseas"?
    (A) He cannot answer a question.
    (B) He is interested in a job offer.
    (C) He should not be blamed for a mistake.
    (D) He is nervous about a change.

48. (　　) What does the woman say a mobile app is used for?
    (A) Personal budgeting.
    (B) Social networking.
    (C) Shopping.
    (D) Global positioning.

49. (　　) What will the woman give the man?
    (A) A staff directory.
    (B) A business card.
    (C) A book.
    (D) A voucher.

M : Hey, Sophia, what are you up to?

W : I'm leading our admin staff meeting today.

M : Oh, I was expecting Aaron. Is he coming, too?

W : Aaron has to attend a meeting at district headquarters.

M : I see. So what's the meeting about?

GO ON TO THE NEXT PAGE.

W : Mainly about the renovations to the East Annex at the beginning of next month. Since the construction company will be moving floor-by-floor, we'll have to move some classes to different rooms while the work is being done.

50. (　　) Where do the speakers most likely work?
    (A) At a school.
    (B) At a department store.
    (C) At a hotel.
    (D) At a factory.

51. (　　) What does the woman mean when she says, "Aaron has to attend a meeting at district headquarters"?
    (A) A co-worker cannot attend a meeting.
    (B) A deadline will be extended.
    (C) She is assigning an additional supervisor.
    (D) She thinks that more staff should be hired.

52. (　　) What will happen next month?
    (A) A training course will begin.
    (B) Some student interns will arrive.
    (C) Some renovation work will start.
    (D) A team will be reorganized.

Questions 53 through 55 *refer to the following conversation.*

W : Hi, is this the information booth for the flea market? I own an accessories shop in town and I'm looking to purchase some beads for my jewelry.

M : Oh, welcome to the Swanson Flea Market. If you keep walking straight, you'll see the Hopper's Hobbies booth at the end of this row on the right. They should have beads.

W : Great. Thank you for your help. I've never been here before and I wasn't sure where to go.

M : Sure, and actually today is the fifth anniversary of this market. There will be a free music festival tonight to celebrate, rain or shine. The first band will start at 6 p.m.

53. (　　) Where does the conversation take place?
    (A) At a library.
    (B) At a museum.
    (C) At a performing arts center.
    (D) At an outdoor market.

54. (   ) What does the woman thank the man for?
        (A) Buying her a ticket.
        (B) Approving her registration form.
        (C) Giving her directions.
        (D) Finding her a seat.

55. (   ) What is scheduled for later in the day?
        (A) A lecture.
        (B) A concert.
        (C) A beauty contest.
        (D) A cooking demonstration.

Questions 56 through 58 *refer to the following conversation.*

W : Lathrop Music. Can I help you?

M : Hi, I own a small dance studio and I have a couple of loudspeakers that aren't working properly. Do you fix sound equipment?

W : Sure, I can repair those. If you drop them off today, they'll be ready by Friday.

M : Actually, I'm flying to a convention in Baltimore on Friday, so I won't be able to pick them up then. I can stop by on Monday when I return, though.

W : Sounds good. That'll give me more time to work on them.

M : Your shop's at 4912 North Beacon Street, right?

W : That's right, and when you get here, I suggest parking behind the building. There are always plenty of spaces available in that area.

56. (   ) What does the man want the woman to do?
        (A) Validate a parking stub.
        (B) Teach a dance class.
        (C) Listen to some recordings.
        (D) Repair some equipment.

57. (   ) Why is the man unavailable on Friday?
        (A) He will be performing.
        (B) He has a dentist appointment.
        (C) He will be traveling.
        (D) He will be visiting a client.

GO ON TO THE NEXT PAGE.

58. (   ) What does the woman recommend the man do?
    (A) Find a new instructor.
    (B) Park in a specific location.
    (C) Pay with a credit card.
    (D) Speak with a manager.

Questions 59 through 61 _refer to the following conversation._

M : Hi, I'm trying to reach Tiffany Tennant in Personnel.

W : Yes, this is Tiffany.

M : Hello, this is Ray Biebergal from sales and marketing. A new employee, Jeff Robbins, is starting in my department next week. And I'm wondering how many weeks of vacation new hires receive.

W : Four weeks a year. That's one of the topics we'll discuss at the new employee orientation. We hold sessions every Monday at 9 o'clock.

M : Thanks for letting me know. I'll make sure Mr. Robbins attends the session. Does he need to sign up in advance?

W : Yes, but I can take care of his registration right now. Let's see… Jeff Robbins, yes, I have his new employee file right here.

59. (   ) What department is the man trying to reach?
    (A) Personnel.
    (B) Information technology.
    (C) Security.
    (D) Engineering.

60. (   ) What does the man inquire about?
    (A) An insurance claim.
    (B) A parking permit.
    (C) A vacation policy.
    (D) A weekly expense.

61. (   ) What does the woman offer to do?
    (A) Take a message.
    (B) Register an employee.
    (C) Contact a supervisor.
    (D) Reserve a room.

W : Hello, I'd like to wire some money to the Philippines.

M : OK, I can help you with that. Have you completed the form?

W : Yes, here it is. Is $15.50 the correct fee?

M : That's right. You're sending less than $1,000.

W : Great. Also, this transfer is somewhat urgent. I'm really hoping it gets there as soon as possible.

M : Well, international transfers can take up to 7 to 10 business days, but they're usually processed much quicker. You can expect it to arrive in a couple of days.

W : That's reassuring. You know, I'm happy your shop has this service. You're right up the block from my house. So, it's really convenient.

M : I'm glad we can help.

62. (   ) Look at the graphic. What information does the woman have a question about?
   (A) The fee.
   (B) The transaction code.
   (C) The date.
   (D) The recipient.

Sender	Gwen Finch
Recipient	Joaquin Rizal
Date	September 22
Amount Sent	$900 US = $46,139 PHP
Fee	$15.50 US
Transaction Code	DT-01238

63. (   ) What is the woman concerned about?
   (A) Who can sign for a delivery.
   (B) What identification is required.
   (C) Where a package can be picked up.
   (D) When a transfer will arrive.

64. (   ) What does the woman say about the shop?
   (A) It has a new owner.
   (B) It is close to where she lives.
   (C) It will have a sales event.
   (D) It has been closed recently.

GO ON TO THE NEXT PAGE.

W : Hello, I manage an office complex and I'm calling about the magnolia trees your nursery sells. I think they would make the grounds look very attractive. I'm looking at your website now.

M : Sure, do you see our tree size chart?

W : Yes, what's the difference between the two smaller types?

M : Type A trees are for planting in pots on balconies or patios. Type B trees produce more flowers but have to be planted in the ground.

W : Hmm, I want to plant them around the buildings. Pots are not an option. Do you deliver?

M : Of course, and we can also plant them for you for an additional $50 per tree.

65. (   ) Why does the woman want some trees?
    (A) To improve the appearance of an area.
    (B) To have a regular supply of flowers.
    (C) To conduct some scientific research.
    (D) To provide more privacy for a home.

66. (   ) Look at the graphic. What size trees does the woman choose?
    (A) 24 inches.
    (B) 36 inches.
    (C) 48 inches.
    (D) 60 inches.

Magnolia Tree Size Chart				
Type	**A**	**B**	**C**	**D**
Height	**24"**	**36"**	**48"**	**60"**

67. (   ) What additional service does the man offer the woman?
    (A) Waste management.
    (B) Regular maintenance.
    (C) Tree planting.
    (D) Fruit harvesting.

W : Mr. Greenberg. There's a conference that I'd like to attend in July and I'm wondering if the company would pay for it. The conference is on networking through social media, and I could learn a lot about how to reach a wider client base using social media.

M : I think that would be doable. We're always looking for ways to attract new clients. How much will it be?

W : I have the fee list here. You know, if I sign up today, I'll get the early registration discount.

M : Right… Um, why don't you go ahead and sign up? I'm curious to know what topics will be covered at the conference.

W : I've got all the information about times and topics. I'll send it to you in an e-mail.

68. (   ) What department does the woman most likely work in?
    (A) Product development.
    (B) Information Technology.
    (C) Sales and Marketing.
    (D) Finance and Accounting.

69. (   ) Look at the graphic. How much will the company most likely pay?
    (A) $1,700.
    (B) $2,200.
    (C) $2,300.
    (D) $2,900.

NATIONAL NETWORKING CONFERNCE

REGISTRATION FEES

	Early (before June 15)	Standard (after June 15)
Students	$1,700	$2,200
Professionals	$2,300	$2,900

70. (   ) What will the woman send the man in an e-mail?
    (A) A confirmation number.
    (B) A cashier's check.
    (C) A travel request form.
    (D) A conference schedule.

GO ON TO THE NEXT PAGE.

PART 4

Good afternoon and welcome to today's Internet literacy seminar. We are pleased to offer this seminar to all Tuscon Public Library patrons who want to improve their online experience. The library has recently purchased some new laptop computers here in the media center. And we're fortunate to have exclusive use of them today. Let's start our seminar by creating a user account for the TPL system—if you don't already have one. Your username will be the bar-code number which is found on the back of your card. For the password, however, please choose a word or phrase that you can easily remember.

71. (   ) What is the topic of the seminar?
    (A) Computer programming.
    (B) Graphic design.
    (C) Buying a used vehicle.
    (D) Using the Internet.

72. (   ) What change did the library recently make?
    (A) It purchased new computers.
    (B) It extended its hours.
    (C) It added a new media center.
    (D) It reduced late fees.

73. (   ) What are listeners asked to do?
    (A) Apply for a card.
    (B) Complete a survey.
    (C) Create an account.
    (D) Select a desktop theme.

Hi, Ms. Chavez. This is Mike Renner calling from Amplify Communications. You've contracted us to set up a wireless network in your office, so your employees will have more flexible Internet access. However, according to the information you submitted to us, it looks like you have 30 employees scattered across two floors. The network we agreed to install doesn't have enough bandwidth to accommodate that many simultaneous Internet users. Considering your tight budget, there are other network options that might work for you. So please give me a call and we can discuss them.

74. (   ) Where does the speaker most likely work?
    (A) At a fitness center.
    (B) At a wireless network provider.
    (C) At a paper supplier.
    (D) At an office furniture store.

75. (   ) What is the purpose of the message?
    (A) To file a complaint.
    (B) To offer an estimate.
    (C) To suggest another service option.
    (D) To ask for more time to complete a project.

76. (   ) What does the speaker ask Ms. Chavez to do?
    (A) Send a fax.
    (B) Sign a contract.
    (C) Return a phone call.
    (D) Submit a deposit.

Questions 77 through 79 *refer to the following telephone message.*

Hello, Mr. Bailey. This is Marcel from D&T Farber. I'm calling about your personal income tax return. I think I may have figured out why the numbers weren't quite matching up. I found two deductions missing from your calculations, which I was able to fix relatively quickly. I'd like to meet with you in person though so that we can discuss the tax credit for which you are now eligible. I've already committed to helping other clients tomorrow but if you're free on Tuesday, I can stop by your office in the afternoon. Please call me back to let me know if that works for you. Thanks.

77. (   ) Who most likely is the speaker?
    (A) A court reporter.
    (B) An architect.
    (C) An accountant.
    (D) A yoga instructor.

GO ON TO THE NEXT PAGE.

78. (   ) What would the speaker like to discuss?
    (A) Reducing company spending.
    (B) Utilizing office space effectively.
    (C) Adjusting a tax return.
    (D) Drafting a product proposal.

79. (   ) What does the speaker say he will do tomorrow?
    (A) Take a vacation day.
    (B) Attend a seminar.
    (C) Meet with clients.
    (D) Mail some forms.

Questions 80 through 82 _refer to the following announcement._

Hey, guys. We just got word from quality assurance that there are some issues with the bikes we assembled this morning. The frames are slightly bent. It seems to be a problem with a limited number of frames in one shipment, so we've got someone taking measurements on the lot. We are obviously unable to operate normally until this problem is resolved and it's just about lunch time. Therefore, we'll break early and take an extra hour. When we come back down on the production floor at 2:00 p.m., we'll hopefully be able to carry on as usual.

80. (   ) Where is this announcement most likely being made?
    (A) At an art gallery.
    (B) At a department store.
    (C) At an appliance warehouse.
    (D) At a bicycle factory.

81. (   ) What problem does the speaker mention?
    (A) Some customers have complained.
    (B) Some materials are faulty.
    (C) A shipment has not arrived.
    (D) A business has opened late.

82. (   ) What are the listeners told to do?
    (A) Come in early tomorrow.
    (B) Print more copies of a flyer.
    (C) Take a longer lunch break.
    (D) Contact a manager.

One last announcement before we close the meeting. I'd like to tell you about a new fundraiser that's being organized by one of our co-workers, Lee Van Vliet. After learning that our local community center was in need of funding, Lee decided to help out by raising some money. So this week only, a donation box will be placed in the cafeteria during lunch. And any amount that you're willing to give will be greatly appreciated. Lee has asked the representative from the community center to come to our next meeting to talk about how funds will be used to benefit the center.

83. (   ) What does the speaker ask the listeners to participate in?
   (A) A fund-raising activity.
   (B) A company picnic.
   (C) A training workshop.
   (D) A community art festival.

84. (   ) What will be available in the cafeteria this week?
   (A) Healthy menu choices.
   (B) Special desserts.
   (C) A donation box.
   (D) A sign-up sheet.

85. (   ) What does the speaker say about the next meeting?
   (A) New employees will be introduced.
   (B) Attendance will be required.
   (C) It will be in a different location.
   (D) A guest will speak.

This morning, another regional hospital announced that it will be closing its mobile health clinic indefinitely. The mobile clinic was designed to improve access to quality health care for people living in the rural areas outside of the city. According to a spokesperson, the hospital ran a mobile health clinic for ten years until forced to shut it down because of budget cutbacks. As budgets for health care are being slashed across the state, authorities are concerned about rural health care, as fewer people will have access to quality services.

GO ON TO THE NEXT PAGE.

86. (   ) According to the news report, what type of facility is being closed?
  (A) A vocational school.
  (B) A bus station.
  (C) A medical clinic.
  (D) A community center.

87. (   ) Why was the facility closed?
  (A) It was outdated.
  (B) Its program was not popular.
  (C) Its funding was eliminated.
  (D) It was in a remote location.

88. (   ) According to the news report, what do authorities fear will happen in the future?
  (A) More people will lack adequate health care.
  (B) Public transportation will improve.
  (C) The income of rural workers will increase.
  (D) Similar services will open in other areas.

Questions 89 through 91 _refer to the following advertisement._

Looking for an Italian restaurant that specializes in traditional Sicilian foods? Then come visit us at Trattoria di Palermo opening soon on West Pico Blvd. Our menu features the famous Sicilian cuisine. All of our unique dishes are prepared from recipes passed down for generations. The restaurant's opening celebration will take place on October 10 from 5:00 p.m. to 10:00 p.m. There'll be food samples and live music. The first 50 guests will be given a free laminated map of Sicily with the Trattoria di Palermo logo. For more information, visit our website at www.trattoriadipalermo.com.

89. (   ) What is special about the restaurant?
  (A) Its location.
  (B) Its service.
  (C) Its food.
  (D) Its design.

90. (   ) According to the speaker, what will happen on October 10?
  (A) A grand opening will take place.
  (B) A major renovation will start.
  (C) A new chef will start work.
  (D) A cooking class will be offered.

91. (   ) What will some guests receive?
   (A) Memberships.
   (B) Calendars.
   (C) T-shirts.
   (D) Maps.

Questions 92 through 94 *refer to the following speech.*

You all deserve a big round of applause today for your hard work in developing the advertising campaign for our longtime client, Pointier Hotel Group. This campaign introducing the group's new chain of boutique hotels was very innovative. For the first time, we created advertisements on social networking sites as well. The ads we created for these sites were particularly effective. Pointier has reported that online bookings have increased by 200% since the campaign started. This indicates that people are reading the online ads and following the website link to learn more about staying in one of their hotels. Our clients are thrilled about this increase, and so am I. Thank you to the entire team for your continued contributions to our company's success.

92. (   ) What type of business was the advertising campaign designed for?
   (A) A bank.
   (B) A hotel group.
   (C) A real estate agency.
   (D) A restaurant chain.

93. (   ) According to the speaker, what was different about the advertising campaign?
   (A) A celebrity was hired to endorse a product.
   (B) A promotional period was extended.
   (C) Ads were posted on social networking sites.
   (D) Coupons were sent by mobile phone.

94. (   ) According to the speaker, what indicates that the advertising campaign was a success?
   (A) Positive survey results.
   (B) Product sample requests.
   (C) Increased foot traffic in retail.
   (D) More website bookings.

GO ON TO THE NEXT PAGE.

You're tuned to KTJB radio. In our last local news story of the hour, the Stanton city council met yesterday to approve a budget for street light improvements in the city's commercial area. City business owners have been petitioning the city council for the past two years to install 200 additional streetlights in the downtown area. They believe that the better lighting will encourage business after dark. In an interview this morning, city council president Robert Miller reported that the estimated cost of the street lights will be about five hundred thousand dollars.

95. (   ) What is the purpose of the broadcast?
    (A) To advertise a store opening.
    (B) To report traffic conditions.
    (C) To remind listeners of an election.
    (D) To announce a city council decision.

96. (   ) What did local business owners request?
    (A) A new parking structure.
    (B) Additional street lights.
    (C) An alternate date for an event.
    (D) An advertising campaign.

97. (   ) Look at the graphic. What will the speaker most likely talk about next?
    (A) Today's top headlines.
    (B) The estimated cost of a construction project.
    (C) Names of newly elected officials.
    (D) Traffic conditions.

KTJB Morning Schedule
(9:15-10:00)

9:15	Headline news
9:20	Business report
9:30	Local news
9:35	Traffic update

Hi, Joseph. This is Maureen. I'm supposed to meet with our sales representatives tomorrow morning and give them a presentation about the changes in our pricing. But unfortunately, I'm not feeling well and I don't think I'll be able to make it to the office tomorrow. So, I was wondering if you would mind taking over for me. I just e-mailed you the slides and notes for the presentation. Feel free to call me with any questions after you have a look at the attachments. Thank you so much.

98. (   ) Why is the woman unable to come to the office tomorrow?
   (A) She will be at a conference.
   (B) She has a sales appointment.
   (C) She is feeling ill.
   (D) She is expecting visitors.

99. (   ) What does the woman ask Joseph to do?
   (A) Give a presentation.
   (B) Postpone an event.
   (C) Verify some prices.
   (D) Consult a colleague.

100. (   ) Please look at the graphic. In what order will Joseph give a presentation at the meeting?
   (A) First.
   (B) Second.
   (C) Third.
   (D) Fourth.

Sales Representative Meeting Agenda

Opening talk — Jeff

Marketing budget — Harry

Price increases — Maureen

Quarterly outlook — Diane

GO ON TO THE NEXT PAGE.

NO TEST MATERIAL ON THIS PAGE

New TOEIC Speaking Test

Question 1: Read a Text Aloud

 **Question 1**

Directions: In this part of the test, you will read aloud the text on the screen. You will have 45 seconds to prepare. Then you will have 45 seconds to read the text aloud.

A meeting of the Zapmeto Board of Directors has been scheduled for 9:00 A.M. on Friday, April 2, at our headquarters. You may join us online if you are unable to attend in person. The first item on the agenda will be to approve the list of planned expenditures for the upcoming month. As most of these are routine, the vote can be held immediately upon gathering. Following this vote, we will take an in-depth look at a proposal to move the assembly lines for several Zapmeto products to the Lexington plant.

PREPARATION TIME
00 : 00 : 45

RESPONSE TIME
00 : 00 : 45

GO ON TO THE NEXT PAGE.

Question 2: Read a Text Aloud

 **Question 2**

Directions: In this part of the test, you will read aloud the text on the screen. You will have 45 seconds to prepare. Then you will have 45 seconds to read the text aloud.

Whether or not you should call in sick because you have a cold depends on its severity. If you are rapidly emptying boxes of tissues and have an uncontrollable cough, you've got a pretty bad cold. You will have trouble concentrating and will likely spread germs to others. If your cold is not that severe and you must go to work, wash your hands frequently and keep your phone and computer germ-free by wiping them down with alcohol wipes if others use them. If your co-workers keep their distance, don't be offended. It may not be the garlic dill you had with lunch, but instead their fear of catching what you have.

PREPARATION TIME
00 : 00 : 45

RESPONSE TIME
00 : 00 : 45

Question 3: Describe a Picture

((◖ 5 ◗)) **Question 3**

Directions: In this part of the test, you will describe the picture on your screen in as much detail as you can. You will have 30 seconds to prepare your response. Then you will have 45 seconds to speak about the picture.

PREPARATION TIME
00 : 00 : 30

RESPONSE TIME
00 : 00 : 45

GO ON TO THE NEXT PAGE.

Question 3: Describe a Picture

答題範例

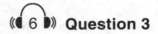 **Question 3**

This is a picture of some people in the parking lot of a department store.

There are three men and one woman.

The woman is pushing a shopping cart.

The shopping cart contains a couple of shopping bags.

The woman has just purchased some things.

She seems pleased with herself.

The two men on the right are wearing T-shirts.

The man on the left is wearing a polo shirt.

Two of them have the same logo on their shirts.

The men are most likely employees of the department store.

They are accompanying the woman to her car.

They will probably help the woman load her purchases into her car.

The man on the left looks like a manager type.

He's wearing long pants, too.

The other two look like they're still in college.

I see a couple of people in the background.

I can see the entrance to the department store.

There's at least one other car in the parking lot.

Questions 4-6: Respond to Questions

 **Question 4**

Directions: In this part of the test, you will answer three questions. For each question, begin responding immediately after you hear a beep. No preparation time is provided. You will have 15 seconds to respond to Questions 4 and 5 and 30 seconds to respond to Question 6.

Imagine that a U.S. marketing firm is doing research in your country. You have agreed to participate in a telephone interview about shopping malls.

Question 4

The last time you visited a shopping mall, how much time did you spend in the mall?

Question 5

When you make a purchase at a shopping mall, what do you usually buy?

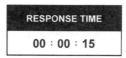

Question 6

Describe one service or policy at your favorite shopping mall that you would like to change.

GO ON TO THE NEXT PAGE.

Questions 4-6: Respond to Questions

答題範例

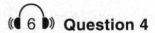 **Question 4**

The last time you visited a shopping mall, how much time did you spend in the mall?

Answer

> I visited the mall about a week ago.
>
> The Galleria on La Brea Avenue.
>
> I spent about an hour in the mall.

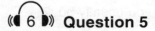 **Question 5**

When you make a purchase at a shopping mall, what do you usually buy?

Answer

> I mostly buy clothing.
>
> Sometimes I buy accessories.
>
> And I eat in the food court sometimes.

Questions 4-6: Respond to Questions

 **Question 6**

Describe one service or policy at your favorite shopping mall that you would like to change.

Answer

I wish there was a private customer lounge.

I've seen them in other high-end malls.

They're like the frequent flyer clubs at the airport.

The lounge has clean restrooms and places to sit.

There's a place for breastfeeding and changing diapers.

They have a little bar where you can buy a drink.

You pay a membership fee for access.

It's good for taking a break.

I know a lot of people who spend hours at the mall.

GO ON TO THE NEXT PAGE.

Questions 7-9: Respond to Questions Using Information Provided

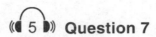 **Question 7**

Directions: In this part of the test, you will answer three questions based on the information provided. You will have 30 seconds to read the information before the questions begin. For each question, begin responding immediately after you hear a beep. No additional preparation time is provided. You will have 15 seconds to respond to Questions 7 and 8 and 30 seconds to respond to Question 9.

Hi, I'm interested in the teacher certification. Would you mind if I asked a few questions?

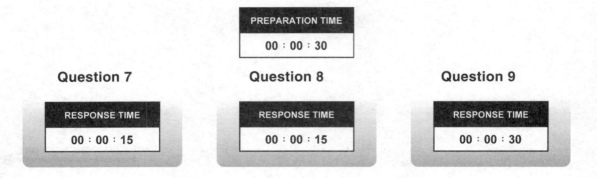

PREPARATION TIME
00 : 00 : 30

Question 7	Question 8	Question 9
RESPONSE TIME	RESPONSE TIME	RESPONSE TIME
00 : 00 : 15	00 : 00 : 15	00 : 00 : 30

Questions 7-9: Respond to Questions Using Information Provided

答題範例

 **Question 7**

What are the main requirements for teacher certification?

Answer

> A bachelor's degree from a regionally accredited school.
>
> A passing score on a state teacher exam.
>
> Completion of an approved teacher training program.

 **Question 8**

Do all teachers need to be certified?

Answer

> In some states, substitute teachers and teacher aides do
>
> not need to be certified.
>
> Most private school teachers are not required to hold a
>
> teaching license.
>
> However, all public school teachers must be certified.

GO ON TO THE NEXT PAGE.

Questions 7-9: Respond to Questions Using Information Provided

 **Question 9**

What is the difference between provisional and standard teaching certifications?

Answer

> The provisional certificate is a temporary license granted to many new teachers.
>
> It allows a teacher to work in the state system.
>
> It's only valid for a limited amount of time.
>
> Teachers on a provisional certificate have not completed the training course.
>
> They may or may not have passed the exam.
>
> It's assumed they will eventually earn a standard teaching license.
>
> The standard license is earned after several years of teaching under a provisional license.
>
> Additionally, all other requirements must be met.
>
> I hope that answers your question.

Question 10: Propose a Solution

 **Question 10**

Directions: In this part of the test, you will be presented with a problem and asked to propose a solution. You will have 30 seconds to prepare. Then you will have 60 seconds to speak. In your response, be sure to show that you recognize the problem, and propose a way of dealing with the problem.

In your response, be sure to

- show that you recognize the caller's problem, and
- propose a way of dealing with the problem.

PREPARATION TIME

00 : 00 : 30

RESPONSE TIME

00 : 01 : 00

GO ON TO THE NEXT PAGE.

Question 10: Propose a Solution

答題範例

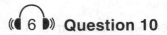 **Question 10**

Voice Message

Hello, this is Trisha from Ann Arbor Farms. We placed an order with your company for 1,500 boxes for transporting strawberries. Because of the bad weather this week, we're going to need the boxes earlier than expected. I'm sorry to change the delivery date for our order at this stage, but I don't have a choice—we'll lose the strawberries if we can't box them as soon as they're harvested. I don't want to call a different supplier. Please let me know whether you'll be able to accommodate the new delivery date for our order.

Question 10: Propose a Solution

答題範例

Hi, Trisha, I got your message.

I understand that you need the boxes sooner than originally
   requested.

I also recognize the urgency of your situation.

We want to do everything we can to keep your business.

We don't want you to look for another supplier.

We will do whatever it takes.

The bad weather has also hampered our deliveries.

We're actually behind schedule on a number of orders.

Everybody is feeling the squeeze.

Meanwhile, I have an idea.

I could ship half of your order today.

It would arrive sometime tomorrow.

And then, I could ship the other half by the end of the week.

You won't lose any strawberries.

So, I think that would be the best course of action.

Let me know if this works.

Let me know if you have other questions.

Give me a call.

GO ON TO THE NEXT PAGE.

Question 11: Express an Opinion

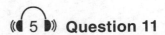 **Question 11**

Directions: In this part of the test, you will give your opinion about a specific topic. Be sure to say as much as you can in the time allowed. You will have 15 seconds to prepare. Then you will have 60 seconds to speak.

Some people crave routine in their daily lives while others thrive on change. What is your opinion about this? Give reasons for your opinion.

PREPARATION TIME
00 : 00 : 15

RESPONSE TIME
00 : 01 : 00

Question 11: Express an Opinion

答題範例

 **Question 11**

> ***Well, I think everybody is a little different.***
>
> I know both types of people.
>
> I also know people who are a mix of both.
>
> Routine is more important in some areas of life than others.
>
> You want public transportation to run on time, every time.
>
> But you don't want to eat the same thing for lunch every single day.
>
> Routine can be a positive experience at work.
>
> Having the muscle memory of an activity makes it much easier to do.
>
> You're less likely to make a mistake.
>
> ***On the other hand, I'm easily bored.***
>
> I can't stand doing the same thing over and over again.
>
> I need variety in my daily tasks.
>
> Like routine, the importance of change varies.
>
> You want to see and do new things as often as possible.
>
> But you don't want to quit a steady job on a whim.
>
> Change is good up until it causes unexpected suffering.
>
> Routine is positive as long as you're in control of what you're doing.
>
> Both have strengths and drawbacks.

GO ON TO THE NEXT PAGE.

NO TEST MATERIAL ON THIS PAGE

New TOEIC Writing Test

Questions 1-5: Write a Sentence Based on a Picture

Question 1

Directions: Write ONE sentence based on the picture using the TWO words or phrases under it. You may change the forms of the words and you may use them in any order.

attend / conference

答題範例：**Some people are attending a conference.**

GO ON TO THE NEXT PAGE.

Questions 1-5: Write a Sentence Based on a Picture

Question 2

Directions: Write ONE sentence based on the picture using the TWO words or phrases under it. You may change the forms of the words and you may use them in any order.

witness / lawyer

答題範例：**The lawyer is questioning the witness.**

Questions 1-5: Write a Sentence Based on a Picture

Question 3

Directions: Write ONE sentence based on the picture using the TWO words or phrases under it. You may change the forms of the words and you may use them in any order.

diver / board

答題範例：**The diver is on the board.**

GO ON TO THE NEXT PAGE.

Questions 1-5: Write a Sentence Based on a Picture

Question 4

Directions: Write ONE sentence based on the picture using the TWO words or phrases under it. You may change the forms of the words and you may use them in any order.

pilot / cockpit

答題範例：**Two pilots are in the cockpit.**

Questions 1-5: Write a Sentence Based on a Picture

Question 5

Directions: Write ONE sentence based on the picture using the TWO words or phrases under it. You may change the forms of the words and you may use them in any order.

write / ticket

答題範例：**The officer is writing a ticket.**

GO ON TO THE NEXT PAGE.

Questions 6-7: Respond to a written request

Question 6

Directions: Read the e-mail below.

From: c_lemm@encoremineral.com
To: p_foster@kmail.com
Subject: Orientation Program
Date: October 3

Dear Mr. Foster,

You are invited to attend the new employee orientation program on October 19. The company's policies and procedures will be covered as well as the services and benefits offered to employees.

Please note that part-time employees like you are also required to attend the meeting. The session will take place in the conference room of the Core Building and will run from 8 A.M. to 1 P.M. Lunch will be served afterward in the cafeteria of the Mantle Building.

Before the orientation, please review the employee handbook that has been provided to you because it will form the basis of the session.

If you are unable to attend the meeting, please notify the Human Resources representative assigned to your department, Ms. Lauren DeBenedictus, as soon as possible. Ms. DeBenedictus can be reached at extension 3210 or at p_debenedictus@emh.com.

We look forward to seeing you.

Sincerely,
Carly Lemm
Assistant Director, Human Resources Department
Encore Mineral Holdings

Directions: Write to Ms. DeBenedictus as Paul Foster, the new employee. Apologize for missing the orientation program and give ONE reason why.

Questions 6-7: Respond to a written request

答題範例

Question 6

Dear Ms. DeBenedictus,

On October 19, I was supposed to attend the new employee orientation program. However, I felt ill the night before, and I had to see a doctor. I am happy to submit my doctor's note if needed. Let me know if you require any further details and what other steps I should take to adequately address this issue.

Sincerely,
Paul Foster

GO ON TO THE NEXT PAGE.

Questions 6-7: Respond to a written request

Question 7

Directions: Read the e-mail below.

From: Kenny Gould (k_gould@sharpmail.com)
To: Louise Minter (l_Minter@lauderdalefinancial.com)
Date: Thursday, July 18
Subject: RE: Note from Kenny Gould

Dear Ms. Minter,

Thank you for approving my application to join your internship program as a stock analyst trainee at Lauderdale Financial. I very much look forward to working at your firm, and I hope that I will be one of the interns you select for a full-time position when the internship ends.

My only concern is that I am currently enrolled in a six-week intensive course called Principles of Market Volatility, which runs until Friday, July 29. Because the internship at your bank begins on Wednesday, July 27, I would need to miss the first three days. Would it be possible for me to start on the following Monday instead? I believe this course will assist me in my work as a stock analyst intern, so I hope that you will still allow me to take advantage of the internship opportunity.

I look forward to your reply.

Sincerely,
Kenny Gould

Directions: Reply to Mr. Gould as Louise Minter, the director of the internship program. Offer ONE solution to Mr. Gould's problem.

Questions 6-7: Respond to a written request

答題範例

Question 7

Hi, Kenny,

Thank you for your e-mail. Your course sounds interesting, and it is certainly relevant to our industry. You will want to know that, because there were so many applicants for the internship positions this year, we decided to offer two month-long internship sessions instead of one. The July 27 session will be first; the second will begin on August 3 and wrap up on August 28. This should alleviate any scheduling conflict.

Regarding full-time paid positions, we'll decide which interns to hire on a permanent basis only after both sessions are over. We will make those decisions by September. These positions have a start date of September 15.

Please call me so we can finalize your plans.

Regards,
Louise Minter

GO ON TO THE NEXT PAGE.

Questions 8: Write an opinion essay

Question 8

Directions: Read the question below. You have 30 minutes to plan, write, and revise your essay. Typically, an effective response will contain a minimum of 300 words.

Do you agree or disagree with the following statement?

Schools should require that students learn how to play a musical instrument. Do you agree? Use specific reasons and examples to explain your answer.

Questions 8: Write an opinion essay

答題範例

Question 8

My short answer to the question is: No, students should not be required to learn a musical instrument.

When I was growing up, music was not compulsory; however, I joined the school band in first grade, and eventually learned to play the piano, drums, and guitar. Music came easily because I loved to play more than anything else. On the other hand, I hated chess, history, and anything related to math. Of course, I was forced to study math along with chemistry and all the other subjects I didn't care about. To be honest, I still hate math, I never use it, and I've got no business in a scientific laboratory. If anything, forcing me to learn algebra and calculus just made me resentful. It's one thing to expose kids to things like music, art, dance, and theater; it's quite another to force it upon them. I don't think it works in the long run as a positive influence.

In a well-rounded system, students are exposed to a wide range of subjects and disciplines, especially the arts. Research has suggested that learning a musical instrument is beneficial to a child's brain development. It's said that music makes you smarter, happier, and more productive. Although listening to music is good, actively playing musical instruments is even more useful for learning cognitive skills.

There is no denying the benefits of playing a musical instrument. Yet, it can't be forced on someone with any more success than forcing mathematics on me was. Most music enthusiasts see playing an instrument as a stress reliever, but for students who are not musically inclined, it's just another thing to worry about. What's more, providing compulsory music lessons to students who have no interest in them—or any kind of arts for that matter—would not help them at all. I shake my head when I think of how much money my parents wasted on a math tutor for me. I was never going to get it.

Students should choose to learn something they care about. Otherwise, they won't be motivated and will eventually lose interest. This kind of learning brings a lot of negativity into a kid's life. Besides, if the music program was not subsidized by the government (read: tax dollars), it would create an unnecessary burden. Buying a musical instrument costs a lot of money and students from low-income families would not be able to afford it. Their parents might have to borrow money, which leads to greater stress on the family.

The current situation doesn't need to be changed. Students can try several instruments without feeling the pressure to master one. Hence, I believe it would be unwise to make it compulsory for students to learn a musical instrument.

TOEIC 練習測驗答案紙

LISTENING SECTION

Part 1

No.	ANSWER
1	A B C D
2	A B C D
3	A B C D
4	A B C D
5	A B C D
6	A B C D
7	A B C D
8	A B C D
9	A B C D
10	A B C D

Part 2

No.	ANSWER	No.	ANSWER
11	A B C	21	A B C
12	A B C	22	A B C
13	A B C	23	A B C
14	A B C	24	A B C
15	A B C	25	A B C
16	A B C	26	A B C
17	A B C	27	A B C
18	A B C	28	A B C
19	A B C	29	A B C
20	A B C	30	A B C

Part 3

No.	ANSWER	No.	ANSWER	No.	ANSWER
31	A B C D	41	A B C D	51	A B C D
32	A B C D	42	A B C D	52	A B C D
33	A B C D	43	A B C D	53	A B C D
34	A B C D	44	A B C D	54	A B C D
35	A B C D	45	A B C D	55	A B C D
36	A B C D	46	A B C D	56	A B C D
37	A B C D	47	A B C D	57	A B C D
38	A B C D	48	A B C D	58	A B C D
39	A B C D	49	A B C D	59	A B C D
40	A B C D	50	A B C D	60	A B C D

Part 4

No.	ANSWER	No.	ANSWER	No.	ANSWER
61	A B C D	71	A B C D	81	A B C D
62	A B C D	72	A B C D	82	A B C D
63	A B C D	73	A B C D	83	A B C D
64	A B C D	74	A B C D	84	A B C D
65	A B C D	75	A B C D	85	A B C D
66	A B C D	76	A B C D	86	A B C D
67	A B C D	77	A B C D	87	A B C D
68	A B C D	78	A B C D	88	A B C D
69	A B C D	79	A B C D	89	A B C D
70	A B C D	80	A B C D	90	A B C D

No.	ANSWER
91	A B C D
92	A B C D
93	A B C D
94	A B C D
95	A B C D
96	A B C D
97	A B C D
98	A B C D
99	A B C D
100	A B C D

READING SECTION

Part 5

No.	ANSWER	No.	ANSWER	No.	ANSWER
101	A B C D	111	A B C D	121	A B C D
102	A B C D	112	A B C D	122	A B C D
103	A B C D	113	A B C D	123	A B C D
104	A B C D	114	A B C D	124	A B C D
105	A B C D	115	A B C D	125	A B C D
106	A B C D	116	A B C D	126	A B C D
107	A B C D	117	A B C D	127	A B C D
108	A B C D	118	A B C D	128	A B C D
109	A B C D	119	A B C D	129	A B C D
110	A B C D	120	A B C D	130	A B C D

Part 6

No.	ANSWER	No.	ANSWER
131	A B C D	141	A B C D
132	A B C D	142	A B C D
133	A B C D	143	A B C D
134	A B C D	144	A B C D
135	A B C D	145	A B C D
136	A B C D	146	A B C D
137	A B C D	147	A B C D
138	A B C D	148	A B C D
139	A B C D	149	A B C D
140	A B C D	150	A B C D

Part 7

No.	ANSWER	No.	ANSWER	No.	ANSWER
151	A B C D	161	A B C D	171	A B C D
152	A B C D	162	A B C D	172	A B C D
153	A B C D	163	A B C D	173	A B C D
154	A B C D	164	A B C D	174	A B C D
155	A B C D	165	A B C D	175	A B C D
156	A B C D	166	A B C D	176	A B C D
157	A B C D	167	A B C D	177	A B C D
158	A B C D	168	A B C D	178	A B C D
159	A B C D	169	A B C D	179	A B C D
160	A B C D	170	A B C D	180	A B C D

No.	ANSWER	No.	ANSWER
181	A B C D	191	A B C D
182	A B C D	192	A B C D
183	A B C D	193	A B C D
184	A B C D	194	A B C D
185	A B C D	195	A B C D
186	A B C D	196	A B C D
187	A B C D	197	A B C D
188	A B C D	198	A B C D
189	A B C D	199	A B C D
190	A B C D	200	A B C D